THE EVERLASTING PEAKS

STEWART FALLS

GOOB'S CAVE

LONE PEAK

UNCLE BUD'S PARK

JUMPER'S HOLE

POKEY'S PLACE

THE MEADOW

CHERRY CREEK

LILY'S BURROW

MS. HOOT'S GARDEN

TAGALONG ALLIE'S BURROW

Sammy
and the
Pecan Pie

To my intelligent and abundant son Nathan,
who has always been a best friend to his little brother, Weston

—Sean Covey

For my twin brother, Tracy

—Stacy Curtis

SIMON & SCHUSTER BOOKS FOR YOUNG READERS
An imprint of Simon & Schuster Children's Publishing Division
1230 Avenue of the Americas, New York, New York 10020
Copyright © 2013 by Franklin Covey Co.
All rights reserved, including the right of reproduction in whole or in part in any form.
SIMON & SCHUSTER BOOKS FOR YOUNG READERS is a trademark of Simon & Schuster, Inc.
For information about special discounts for bulk purchases, please contact Simon & Schuster Special Sales at
1-866-506-1949 or business@simonandschuster.com.
The Simon & Schuster Speakers Bureau can bring authors to your live event. For more information or to book an
event, contact the Simon & Schuster Speakers Bureau at 1-866-248-3049 or visit our
website at www.simonspeakers.com.
Book design by Laurent Linn
The text for this book is set in Montara Gothic.
The illustrations for this book are rendered in pencil and watercolor.
Manufactured in China
0617 SCP
4 6 8 10 9 7 5
CIP data for this book is available from the Library of Congress.
ISBN 978-1-4424-7647-9
ISBN 978-1-4424-7648-6 (eBook)

Sammy
and the
Pecan Pie

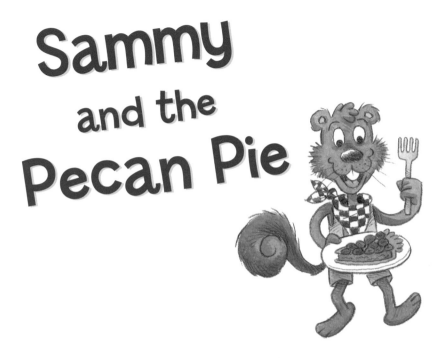

SEAN COVEY
Illustrated by Stacy Curtis

SIMON & SCHUSTER BOOKS FOR YOUNG READERS

New York   London   Toronto   Sydney   New Delhi

Sammy and his twin sister, Sophie, usually got along.

But sometimes he wished she didn't do everything right.

One day at school, Ms. Hoot said, "Ruffle my feathers, Sophie. You got one hundred percent again!"

"And you did a good job too, Sammy," said Ms. Hoot.

I wish I could get one hundred percent like Sophie, thought Sammy.

After school everyone went to Mandy's Candies.

"We have four dollars and fifty cents. How much candy

can we get?" said Lily Skunk.

"A lot," said Goob.

"We can get three bags of yummy gummies, two
chocolate worms, and two lucky suckers," said Sophie.

"Wow, Sophie, you added that up fast," said Goob.

"Yeah, your brain must be huge," said Jumper. "Like as big as a basketball."

"Geez, Sammy, what's it wike to have such a smaht sistuh?" asked Tagalong Allie.

"I dunno." Sammy shrugged. "I guess it's all right," he said as he headed home.

Later that night Sammy and Sophie were with their mom and dad.

"Guess what, Mom?" asked Sophie. "The big spelling bee is coming up."

"Oh, Sophie, you're sure to win! And how about you, Sammy?

Are you going to enter?"

"I guess," Sammy mumbled.

"I've got a special dessert tonight," said Mom. "Pecan pie!"

"That's my favorite!" said Sammy, brightening.

"I hope you like it!" said Mom.

"Why does Sophie always get the bigger piece? She always wins!"

yelled Sammy. Sammy ran to his room and slammed the door.

His mom followed him.

"What's the matter, Sammy?" Mom asked quietly.

"Nothin'," said Sammy.

"C'mon, little squirrel. I know when something's bothering you."

"It's just that Sophie gets all the attention. Everyone thinks she's so smart. And it makes me feel dumb."

"I'm sorry you feel that way, Sammy. But you're smart too!"

"I never get one hundred percent on my spelling tests," said Sammy.

"Maybe not, but Sophie can't build model rockets like you can," said Mom. "Just because Sophie is good at something doesn't take anything away from you."

"What do you mean?" asked Sammy.

"Well, some people think that life is like a pie. If someone gets a big piece, there is less for you. But really, life is more like an all-you-can-eat buffet. Everyone can have all the pie they want. Sophie can have a big piece, and so can you. You can both win."

"So if it's an all-you-can-eat buffet, can I have another piece of pie?"

"Oh, you're such a nut," said Mom.

A few days later it was time for the big science fair.

"Hey, everyone," hollered Sophie. "Come take a look at Sammy's booth! It's phenomenal!"

"Thanks, Sophie," said Sammy. "Yours is good too."

"Wow, Sophie! Your bwuvah is so bwainey!" said Tagalong Allie.

Sammy blushed as Sophie beamed.

"The science fair was a blast today," said Sammy as they
walked home. "I hope Mom has some pie left."

"Yeah, as long as I get the biggest piece," said Sophie, winking
at Sammy.

"I think there's more than enough for both of us," said Sammy.

"Last one home's a rotten egg!"

PARENTS' CORNER

HABIT ④ —Think Win-Win: *Everyone Can Win*

I ADORE MY TWO LITTLE BOYS, NATHAN AND WESTON. THREE YEARS APART, THEY ARE THE best of friends. I'm especially proud of the way they attend each other's sporting events to cheer each other on. Becoming jealous of each other's success never even enters their minds. As far as they're concerned, if one of them succeeds, they both succeed. This is the win-win spirit, the belief that there is more than enough success to go around and to spare.

I hope my boys will always feel this way toward each other and their friends. But I know this won't be easy in this competitive world of ours. As we mature, if we aren't careful, envy and jealousy can creep into our hearts. And it is not uncommon to find ourselves becoming threatened by the successes of others, especially those closest to us, as if their success somehow takes something away from us.

As parents and teachers, there is so much we can do to instill confidence and win-win thinking in our kids. First, we can show unconditional love at all times instead of doling out love based on performance. Next, we can avoid comparative language at all costs, such as, "Why can't you do your homework like your brother?" In its place we can use language that affirms a child's worth and potential, such as, "You're so good at that!"

In this story, point out that, like Sammy, we too need to learn to not be jealous or to compare ourselves to others. The truth is, we are all VIPs. There is something different and special inside of each of us.

Up for Discussion

1. After Sophie got 100% on her test, how did Sammy feel?

2. Of all the candy in Mandy's Candies, which would you like the best?

3. Why did Sammy leave the table unhappy after dinner? What did his mother say to make him feel better?

4. What did Sammy make for the science fair?

5. How did Sophie feel about Sammy doing so well at the science fair? How should you feel when one of your friends does well at something?

Baby Steps

1. Draw a picture of something your best friend is really good at. Now draw a picture of something you're really good at.

2. Do you ever compare yourself to another person? Who is it? Talk to your mom and dad about that.

3. Play a game and don't worry about who wins or loses. Play just for the fun of it.

4. Help a family member do a household chore. Work together to make it go faster.

5. In the next five minutes, compliment a family member on something they do well.